Walt Disney's COWBOY MICKEY

By Cindy West
Illustrated
by Guelle

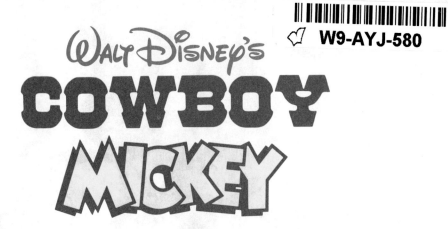

A GOLDEN BOOK • NEW YORK
Western Publishing Company, Inc., Racine, Wisconsin 53404

Mickey Mouse was very busy packing his suitcase.

"Hurry," urged Minnie. "I just can't wait to get to the Lucky Star Dude Ranch!"

"I'm excited, too!" Mickey told her. "I've always wanted to learn how to ride a horse!"

"And I've always wanted to be a cowgirl!" said Minnie.

Just then Goofy raced in with his suitcase. "I'm all packed and ready to go!" he shouted. "I'm going to learn how to ride and to twirl a lasso so I can perform in the Lucky Star Rodeo."

"Is there really going to be a rodeo at the ranch?" asked Minnie.

"That's what I heard," said Mickey. "Wouldn't it be great if we could all be in it?"

"Yes," agreed Minnie. "Let's try."

Goofy couldn't wait to show everyone how well he could ride. The minute he reached the Lucky Star Ranch, he jumped on the first horse he saw. But he jumped on backward!

"Uh-oh!" Goofy gulped. "What do I do now?" He held on tightly to the horse's tail as it leapt around in circles.

Luckily Minnie had brought a bunch of carrots
with her to feed the horses. She held them out to
the horse, and he stopped jumping and whinnied
happily as he trotted over to eat them. Goofy
quickly jumped off the horse.

"Whew! That was really exciting," gasped Goofy.
"Minnie, thanks a lot for showing up with those
carrots."

"It looks like you folks need riding lessons," said the owner of the ranch as he joined them. "Call me Cowboy Bob, and let me show you the right way to get on a horse."

He held the horses' reins as he helped Mickey, Minnie, and Goofy step up and onto their horses.

"Hey, that wasn't hard at all," bragged Goofy. "Now I'm ready to learn how to use a lasso."

"Lassoing takes lots of practice," said Cowboy Bob, and he gave Goofy his first lesson.

That night Mickey and Minnie and some of the ranch hands had a cookout under the stars.

"Yippee-ti-yi-yo!" they all sang around the campfire.

Suddenly they heard a wild cry and saw a strange shadow.

"I think it's a coyote!" whispered Mickey.

Quickly Cowboy Bob shined his flashlight at the shadow.

"It's not a coyote—it's Goofy!" said Minnie with a giggle. "He's walking on his hands and knees!"

"I fooled you, didn't I?" said Goofy, who was laughing and laughing.

The next day Mickey and Minnie practiced
their riding while Goofy practiced with his lasso.

"You're learning very fast," Cowboy Bob told
Mickey and Minnie. "I bet you'll be good enough to
perform in the rodeo."

"How about me?" asked Goofy. "Watch how well
I twirl this lasso.

"Whoops," he cried as he roped his own
foot. "I'd better practice some more."

So while Minnie and Mickey galloped all around the ranch, Goofy tossed his lasso. He tried to rope fences and he tried to rope the Lucky Star sign, but he always ended up roping himself.

Finally the day of the big rodeo arrived, and Cowboy Bob said they could all perform.

"Let's all line up for the grand rodeo parade!" shouted Cowboy Bob.

"Where's Mickey?" asked Minnie. "I haven't seen him anywhere."

"I don't know," said Goofy. "I haven't seen him either."

At that very moment Mickey was asleep! He'd
forgotten to set his alarm clock to wake up in time
for the rodeo. But as crowds passed his window on
their way to the rodeo, their talking woke him.

When Mickey realized how late he'd slept, he
knew he had to hurry or he'd miss the rodeo.

Mickey got dressed as fast as he could and dashed out the door. "I'd better take all the shortcuts I can," he thought as he raced across a field and jumped over a fence.

"Uh-oh," Mickey groaned. "I think maybe I shouldn't have jumped over that fence." Mickey had just landed on a bucking bronco in the middle of the rodeo arena.

Everyone cheered as Mickey held tightly to the reins, riding the bronco. "This is sort of fun!" thought Mickey, and then he waved his hat to the crowd.

"Ladies and gentlemen," called the rodeo announcer, "Mickey Mouse just broke the ranch record for the longest time riding a bronco."

The crowd cheered again.

When Mickey jumped off the bronco, it began to chase him. "What do I do now?" shouted Mickey.

"I'll lasso him for you," yelled Goofy, but he lassoed Mickey instead.

However, seeing Mickey all roped up was such a funny sight, even the bucking bronco stopped for a chuckle.

Then Mickey quickly untied himself and raced away.

Everybody cheered as Cowboy Bob presented the rodeo ribbons.

Minnie won for being the best cowgirl and taking good care of the horses.

Mickey won for his bronco riding.

And Goofy won for trying to lasso anything and everything in sight!

That night everyone sat around the campfire one last time. "This has been the most fun I've ever had," Mickey told Minnie.

"Me, too," she said with a sigh. "I love being a cowgirl."

Just then they all saw an odd profile against the full moon.

"I'll bet it's Goofy joking again," said Mickey.

"Nope! I'm sitting right here," said Goofy.

"Then it's a real coyote!" shouted Mickey. "Now I truly feel like a cowboy. Cowboys and coyotes go together."

"Do you want me to lasso him?" asked Goofy.

"No, thanks," they all said as they laughed.